STEAM TRAIN,
Dream Train

Steam Train, Dream Train

Sherri Duskey Rinker and Tom Lichtenheld

Through the darkness, *clickety-clack* . . .
coming closer, down the track . . .
hold your breath so you can hear
huffing, chuffing drawing near.

A whistle blares
out in the night:
a mighty **engine**—
wondrous sight!

The smokestack puffs, the big wheels grind.

The trusty **tender's** close behind.

Cling! Clang! The bell rings out on top.

Hissing steam. Brakes squeal. Then STOP!

The driver signals
to the crew—
each worker knows
just what to do.
Quick!
Before it gets too late,
start to load up
all the freight.

Everything will
soon be stowed,
a train car matched
to every load.

The crew slides back the **boxcar** doors
and tumbles in to start their chores.
They whirl, twirl, cartwheel, jump,
but cargo's stowed without a bump.

Things that rock and roll and spin,

all are juggled safely in.

The freight is loaded
as they play.
They work—and bounce—
the night away!

Building blocks,
erector sets,
bikes and kites
and model jets—

the **boxcar**'s made
to safely haul
almost
anything at all!

The **hopper**'s top is open wide,
so cargo can be poured inside.
The crew hops to it, one and all—
they get to work and have a ball!

Then with a bounce,

a pounce,

a leap,

three boys jump in . . . and fall asleep.

Tankers, lined up in a row,
are getting filled with paints to go.
Purple, yellow, green, and blue:
a color convoy, coming through.

The **reefer car** is snug and cold.
Its chilly box can safely hold
frozen treats for every stop,
like a rolling ice cream shop!

The train car's packed.
The crew sits back
and chills out with
a midnight snack.

REEFER NO. 1
—
MAX. LOAD:
A MONTH OF
SUNDAES

Ten hard workers lend a hand
to fill the **gondolas** with sand.

Sand for castles,
moats, and more.
Sand for tunnels,
sand galore!

Stacked up on the **autorack**:

six race cars for a private track!

Rainbow colors, flames, and stripes,

shiny engines, chromy pipes.

The autorack

will gently keep

these fast, fast cars . . .

. . . all fast asleep.

The **well cars** carry giant beasts
munching on enormous feasts.
Brachiosaurus likes the view,
while T-rex gets a bone to chew.

The **flatbed cars** are rolling beds.
The weary crew can rest their heads,
and settle in, and tuck in tight.
Their work is finished for tonight.

The red **caboose** is last in line—
from the lookout, all looks fine.

The freight and crew are tucked away.

The next stop . . . is another day.

A hiss, a jolt, a shift and sway,

now the journey's underway.

The train's departing, car by car.

The headlight fades into the stars.

Puffing, chuffing out of sight . . .

Steam train, dream train . . .

chhhhhh . . . goodnight.

To Dave, Ben, and Zak: Thank you for this amazing journey.
To my Dad, Ron Duskey, for a lifetime of love, support,
(mostly!) good advice, and the occasional harsh lecture.
And to my Father, who has led the way —S. D. R.

To my Dad, for being an artist and a gentleman. (And for
buying us *Mad* magazine.)
To my Mom, for encouraging my creativity and—to this
day—showing us what matters. —T. L.

ISBN 978-0-545-78572-3

Text copyright © 2013 by Sherri Duskey Rinker.
Illustrations copyright © 2013 by Tom Lichtenheld.
All rights reserved. Published by Scholastic Inc.,
557 Broadway, New York, NY 10012,
by arrangement with Chronicle Books LLC.
SCHOLASTIC and associated logos are trademarks
and/or registered trademarks of Scholastic Inc.

12 11 10 9 8 7 6 5 4 3 2 1   14 15 16 17 18 19/0

Printed in the U.S.A.   08

This edition first printing, September 2014

Book design by Tom Lichtenheld and Kristine Brogno
Typeset in Neutraface Slab
The illustrations in this book were rendered in
Neocolor wax oil pastels on Mi-Teintes paper.